Maria Edgeworth

The Children's Miscellany

Part IV.: Consisting of Select Stories, Fables, and Dialogues, for...

Maria Edgeworth

The Children's Miscellany
Part IV.: Consisting of Select Stories, Fables, and Dialogues, for...

ISBN/EAN: 9783744767668

Printed in Europe, USA, Canada, Australia, Japan

Cover: Foto ©Andreas Hilbeck / pixelio.de

More available books at **www.hansebooks.com**

THE
Children's Miſcellany;

CONSISTING OF

Select Stories, Fables, and Dialogues,

FOR

The Inſtruction and Amuſement of Young Perſons.

PART IV.

LONDON:

PRINTED FOR THOMAS BLAND, SHEFFIELD;
AND MUNDELL & SON, EDINBURGH.

1796.

CHILDREN'S MISCELLANY.

The Flower Pot.

ROSAMOND, a little girl of about seven
years old, was walking with her mother
in the streets of London. As she passed along,
she looked in at the windows of several shops,
and she saw a great variety of different sorts of
things, of which she did not know the use, or
even the names. She wished to stop to look at
them, but there were a great number of people in the streets, and a great many carts, and
carriages, and wheelbarrows, and she was afraid
to let go her mother's hand.

"Oh! mother, how happy I should be,"
said she, as she passed a toy-shop, "if I had all
these pretty things!"

"What, all! Do you wish for them all,
Rosamond?"

"Yes, mamma, all."

As she spoke they came to a milliner's shop; the windows were hung with ribbons and lace, and festoons of artificial flowers.

" Oh, mamma, what beautiful roses ! Won't you buy some of them ?"

" No, my dear."

" Why ?"

" Because I don't want them, my dear."

They went on a little farther, and they came to another shop, which caught Rosamond's eye. It was a jeweller's shop, and there were a great many pretty baubles, ranged in drawers behind glass.

" Mamma, you'll buy some of these ?"

" Which of them, Rosamond ?"

" Which,—I don't know which ;—but any of them, for they are all pretty."

" Yes, they are all pretty ; but what use would they be of to me ?"

" Use ! Oh, I'm sure you could find some use or other, if you would only buy them first."

" But I would rather find out the ufe firft."

" Well, then, mamma, there are buckles: you know buckles are ufeful things, very ufeful things."

" I have a pair of buckles, I don't want another pair," faid her mother, and walked on. Rofamond was very forry that her mother wanted nothing. Prefently, however, they came to a fhop, which appeared to her far more beautiful than the reft. It was a chemift's fhop, but fhe did not know that.

" Oh, mother ! oh !" cried fhe, pulling her mother's hand; " Look, look, blue, green, red, yellow, and purple ! Oh, mamma, what beautiful things ! Won't you buy fome of thefe ?"

Still her mother anfwered as before; " What ufe would they be of to me, Rofamond ?"

" You might put flowers in them, mamma, and they would look fo pretty on the chimney-piece ;—I wifh I had one of them."

" You have a flower-pot," faid her mother, "—and that is not a flower-pot."

" But I could ufe it for a flower-pot, mamma, you know."

" Perhaps if you were to fee it nearer, if you were to examine it, you might be difappointed."

" No, indeed, I'm fure I fhould not; I fhould like it exceedingly."

Rofamond kept her head turned to look at the purple vafe, till fhe could fee it no longer.

" Then, mother," faid fhe, after a paufe, " perhaps you have no money ."

" Yes, I have."

" Dear, if I had money, I would buy rofes, and boxes, and buckles, and purple flower-pots, and every thing." Rofamond was obliged to paufe in the midft of her fpeech.

" Oh, mamma, would you ftop a minute for me; I have got a ftone in my fhoe, it hurts me very much."

" How comes there to be a ftone in your fhoe ?"

" Becaufe of this great hole, mamma—it

comes in there; my ſhoes are quite worn out; I wiſh you'd be ſo very good as to give me another pair."

" Nay, Roſamond, but I have not money enough to buy ſhoes, and flower-pots, and buckles, and boxes, and every thing."

Roſamond thought that was a great pity. But now her foot, which had been hurt by the ſtone, began to give her ſo much pain that ſhe was obliged to hop every other ſtep, and ſhe could think of nothing elſe. They came to a ſhoemaker's ſhop ſoon afterwards.

" There! there! mamma, there are ſhoes; there are little ſhoes that would juſt fit me; and you know ſhoes would be really of uſe to me."

" Yes, ſo they would, Roſamond.—Come in."—She followed her mother into the ſhop.

Mr. Sole the ſhoemaker had a great many cuſtomers, and his ſhop was full; ſo they were obliged to wait.

" Well, Roſamond," ſaid her mother, " you

don't think this ſhop ſo pretty as the reſt ?"

" No, not nearly ; it's black and dark, and there are nothing but ſhoes all round ; and, be-ſides, there's a very diſagreeable ſmell."

" That ſmell is the ſmell of new leather."

" Is it ?—Oh !" ſaid Roſamond, looking round, " there is a pair of little ſhoes ; they'll juſt fit me, I'm ſure."

" Perhaps they might ; but you cannot be ſure till you have tried them on, any more than you can be quite ſure that you ſhould like the purple vaſe *exceedingly*, till you have exa-mined it more attentively."

" Why, I don't know about the ſhoes cer-tainly, till I've tried ; but, mamma, I am quite ſure I ſhould like the flower-pot.'

" Well, which would you rather have, that jar, or a pair of ſhoes ? I will buy either for you."

" Dear mamma, thank you—but if you could buy both ?"

" No, not both."

" Then the jar if you pleafe."

" But I fhould tell you, that I fhall not give you another pair of fhoes this month."

" This month !—that's a very long time indeed !—You can't think how thefe hurt me; I believe I'd better have the new fhoes—but yet, that purple flower-pot !—Oh, indeed, mamma, thefe fhoes are not fo very, very bad ; I think I might wear them a little longer; and the month will be foon over : I can make them laft till the end of the month; can't I?—Don't you think fo, mamma?"

" Nay, my dear, I want you to think for yourfelf: you will have time enough to confider about it, whilft I fpeak to Mr. Sole about my clogs."

Mr. Sole was by this time at leifure; and whilft her mother was fpeaking to him, Rofamond ftood in profound meditation, with one fhoe on, and the other in her hand.

" Well, my dear, have you decided ?"

" Mamma !—yes,—I believe.—If you pleafe

A 5

—I fhould like the flower-pot; that is, if you won't think me very filly, mamma."

" Why, as to that, I can't promife you, Rofamond; but, when you are to judge for yourfelf, you fho:ld choofe what will make you the happieft; and then it would not fignify who thought you filly."

" Then, mamma, if that's all, I'm fure the flower-pot would make me the happieft," faid fhe, putting on her old fhoe again; " fo I choofe the flower-pot."

" Very well, you fhall have it; clafp your fhoe, and come home."

Rofamond clafped her fhoe, and ran after her mother; it was not long before the fhoe came down at the heel, and many times was fhe obliged to ftop, to take the ftones out of her fhoe, and often was fhe obliged to hop with pain; but ftill the thoughts of the purple flower-pot prevailed, and fhe perfifted in her choice.

When they came to the fhop, with the large

window, Rofamond felt her joy redouble upon hearing her mother defire the fervant, who was with them, to buy the purple jar, and bring it home. He had other commiffions, fo he did not return with them. Rofamond, as foon as fhe got in, ran to gather all her own flowers, which fhe had in a corner of her mother's garden.

" I'm afraid they'll be dead before the flower-pot comes, Rofamond," faid her mother to her when fhe was coming in with the flowers in her lap.

" No, indeed, mamma, it will come home very foon, I dare fay ;—and fhan't I be very happy putting them into the purple flower-pot ?"

" I hope fo, my dear."

The fervant was much longer returning home than Rofamond expeded ; but at length he came, and brought with him the long-wifhed for jar. The moment it was fet down upon the table, Rofamond ran up, with an exclamation

of joy. "I may have it now, mamma?"—
"Yes, my dear, it is your's." Rofamond.
poured the flowers from her lap upon the car-
pet, and feized the purple flower-pot.

"Oh, dear mother!" cried fhe, as foon as
fhe had taken off the top, "but there's fomething dark in it—it fmells very difagreeably
—what is it? I didn't want this black ftuff."

"Nor I neither, my dear."

"But what fhall I do with it, mamma?"

"That I cannot tell."

"But it will be of no ufe to me, mamma."

"That I can't help."

"But I muft pour it out, and fill the flower-
pot with water."

"That's as you pleafe, my dear."

"Will you lend me a bowl to pour it into,
mamma?"

"That was more than I promifed you, my
dear, but I will lend you a bowl"

The bowl was produced, and Rofamond pro-
ceeded to empty the purple vafe. But what

was her furprife and difappointment, when it was entirely empty, to find that it was no long-er a *purple* vafe. It was a plain white glafs jar, which had appeared to have that beautiful colour, merely from the liquor with which it had been filled.

Little Rofamond burft into tears.

" Why fhould you cry, my dear?" faid her mother; it will be of as much ufe to you now, as ever, for a flower-pot."

" But it won't look fo pretty on the chimney-piece:—I am fure, if I had known that it was not really purple, I fhould not have wifhed to have it fo much."

" But didn't I tell you that you had not ex-amined it; and that perhaps you would be dif-appointed?"

" And fo I am difappointed, indeed; I wifh I had believedyou beforehand. Now I had much rather have the fhoes; for I fhall not be able to walk all this month : even walking home that little way hurt me exceedingly.

Mamma, I'll give you the flower-pot back again, and that purple stuff and all, if you'll only give me the shoes."

" No, Rosamond, you must abide by your own choice; and now the best thing you can possibly do is, to bear your disappointment with good humour."

" I will bear it as well as I can," said Rosamond, wiping her eyes; and she began slowly and sorrowfully to fill the vase with flowers.

But Rosamond's disappointment did not end here; many were the difficulties and distresses into which her imprudent choice brought her, before the end of the month. Every day her shoes grew worse and worse, till at last she could neither run, dance, jump or walk in them. Whenever Rosamond was called to see any thing, she was pulling her shoes up at the heels, and was sure to be too late. Whenever her mother was going out to walk, she could not take Rosamond with her, for Rosamond had no soles to her shoes; and, at length, on the very laſt day of the month, it happened, that her father propoſed to take her with her brother to a glaſs-houſe, which ſhe had long wiſhed to ſee. She was very happy; but, when ſhe was quite ready, had her hat and gloves on, and was making haſte down ſtairs to her brother and her father, who were waiting at the hall-door for her, the ſhoe dropped off; ſhe put it on again in a great hurry, but, as ſhe was going acroſs the hall, her father turned round. " Who is that who is walking ſlip-ſhod ? no one muſt walk ſlip-ſhod with me; why, Roſamond, ſaid he, looking at her ſhoes with diſguſt, I thought that you were always neat; go, I cannot take you with me."

Roſamond coloured and retired.—" Oh, mamma, ſaid ſhe," as ſhe took off her hat; " how I wiſh that I had choſen the ſhoes—they would have been of ſo much more uſe to me than that jar: however, I am ſure—no, not quite ſure—but, I hope, I ſhall be wiſer another time."

The Vanity of fancying Ourselves too wife to be taught.

THE *Magpye* alone, of all the birds, had the art of building a neft, the form of which was with a covering over head, and only a fmall hole to creep out at.—The reft of the birds, being without houfes, defired the *Pye* to teach them how to build one.—A day is appointed, and they all meet.—The *Pye* then fays, " You muft lay two fticks acrofs, " thus."——" Aye, fays the *Crow*, I thought " that was the way to begin.—Then lay a little " ftraw and mofs——Certainly, fays the *Jack-* " *daw*, I knew that muft follow.—Then place " more ftraw, mofs, and feathers, in fuch a " manner as this.——Aye, without doubt, cries " the *Starling*, that muft necefilarily follow; " any one could tell how to do that."——When the *Pye* had gone on teaching them till the neft was built half way, and every bird in his turn

had known either one thing or another, he left off, and faid, " Gentlemen, I find you all un-
" derftand building nefts as well, if not better,
" than I do; therefore you cannot want any
" more of my inftructions."——So faying, he flew away, and left them to upbraid each other with their folly; which is vifible to this day, as no bird but the *Magpye* knows how to build more than half a neft.

The reafon thefe foolifh birds never knew how to build more than half a neft, was, that, inftead of trying to learn what the *Pye* told them, they would boaft of knowing more already than he could teach them: And this fame fate will certainly attend all thofe foolifh children, who had rather pleafe themfelves with the vanity of fancying they are already wife, than take pains to become fo.

MR. Thomas Watkins had two daughters, Miss Hannah and Miss Fanny. Their father and mother assigned them a very pretty apartment for their own use, allowed them all things in great plenty, and only desired them to keep their clothes, linen, and all their things, in such a proper order, that they might have the use of them. But these two foolish girls fancying themselves wiser than their parents, disobeyed their commands, and threw all their things about in such irregular heaps, that whenever they were to be dressed, they found themselves more at a loss, than any poor girl would have been, who had not had half their plenty allowed her. Whenever their mamma sent them word she would take them abroad, they were in the greatest confusion that can be imagined: "Oh! sister Hannah (cries Miss " Fanny), can you tell where I put my cap?"

" No, indeed (anfwers Mifs Hannah), nor can
" I find my own, nor my gloves, nor my hood.
" Well, what fhall I do? My mamma is in
" fuch a hurry, fhe will not ftay for us."——
Then would thefe two girls tumble all the
things in their drawers; but in that confufion could find nothing, till their mamma was
drove from the door, leaving them at home as
they deferved: Whilft, looking afhamed at each
other, they were laughed at by the reft of the
family.

Thus will thofe foolifh children be ferved,
who heap into their heads a great deal, and
yet never obferve what they put there, either
to mend their practice, or increafe their knowledge. Their heads will be in as much confufion, as were Mifs Watkins's chefts of drawers.
And when in company, they endeavour to
find out fomething to fay to the purpofe, they
will be hunting in the midft of a heap of rub-
bifh, whilft they expofe themfelves and become
a laughing-ftock to their companions.

The Work-Houfe Boy.

AS Mrs. Barnet returned from town, the
poſt-chaife broke down in the middle of
the road—a ftage-coach came up at the inftant
that Mrs Barnet and her maid had got fafely
out of the poſt-chaife ; the coachman knew
Mrs. Barnet, and his courfe being directly
through a village contiguous to her hufband's
houfe, he ftopp'd, and offered to fet her down
at her own door.—Mrs. Barnet perceiving that
it would take a confiderable time before the
chaife could be mended, agreed to the coachman's propofal, and defired her maid to put a
fmall bundle into the coach.

" Madam," cried the maid, as foon as fhe
had peeped into the coach, " here is a fright-
" ful old woman and a beggarly looking boy—
" you cannot poffible go in here."

" As for the old woman and the boy," faid
the coachman, " although they are fitting with-

" *in*, they are no more than outside paſſengers
" —for as ill luck would have it, I chanced to
" have none within ; ſo when the rain came
" on, I took pity on the boy, and deſired him
" to take ſhelter in the coach, which he refuſed,
" unleſs the old woman was allowed to go
" in alſo ;—ſo as the boy, you ſee, is a very
" pretty boy, I could not bear that he ſhould
" be expoſed to the rain, and ſo I was obliged
" to let in both ; but now, to be ſure, if her
" ladyſhip inſiſts on it, they muſt both go on
" the outſide, which will be no great hardſhip,
" for it begins to grow fair."

" By no means," ſaid Mrs. Barnet ; " let
" the child remain, and the woman alſo; there
" is room for us all."

So ſaying, ſhe ſtepped into the coach; the
maid followed, and the coachman drove on.

The old woman, being delighted with her
ſituation in the coach, was in high ſpirits, and
began to talk with the boy.

His prattle ſoon attracted the attention of

Mrs. Barnet, who asked the old woman, what relation the boy was to her.

" Relation to me !" answered she. " Please your Ladyship, I never saw him in my life, " till this here blessed day, when I received " him from the overseers of the work-house, " to take him to my own house in the coun- " try; where I already have six children all " boarded at the rate of poor three shillings a " week."

" Pray, who are his parents ?" said Mrs. Barnet, interrupting the old woman's fluency.

" The Lord above, he only knows," replied the old woman; " for they told me he was " brought to the work-house when he was only " a few months old; the parish officers received " him from a poor woman, who said she was " not his mother, but his name was Edward; " but who were his parents is difficult to tell; " for they have never been found out."

Mrs. Barnet, affected with the condition of this boy, who began life under such unfavour-

able aufpices, faid, " Are you not forry, my
" dear, to leave home ?"

" No," anfwered he ; " I dont care."

" Is there not fomebody at home whom you
" are fofry to leave ?" refumed fhe.

" No," replied the boy, " I am not forry to
" leave any body."

" What, not thofe who are good to you ?"
rejoined fhe.

" Nobody was ever good to *me*," faid the
boy.

" My poor little fellow," faid fhe, after a
fhort paufe, " was *nobody* ever good to you ?"

" No," anfwered he, " they are good only
" to the Miftrefs's fon."

" And have you *no* friend, my dear ?" added fhe with a figh.

" No, for old Robin the foot-man died laft
" week."

" Was he your friend ?

" Yes, that he was," replied the boy ; " he
" once gave me a piece of gingerbread.'

Mrs. Barnet could not help fmiling at the expreffive fimplicity of the anfwer, and felt herfelf fo much interefted in him, and fo much affected at feeing fo fine a child thrown as it were at random on the world, that while fhe yet fmiled, the tears flowed from her eyes— which the boy obferving, and miftaking their caufe, faid, " I fell a crying myfelf, when I " heard that poor old Robin was dead."

" That was like a good boy," faid Mrs. Barnet.

" No, it was like a naughty boy," faid he; " and the matron whipt me for it."

" My poor dear little fellow," exclaimed Mrs. Barnet, " that was hard indeed !"

" It is very right howfomever, Madam," faid the old woman, " that children fhould be " whipt for crying ; if I did not make that a " conftant rule at my houfe, there would be " nothing but fquawling from morning to night " —for I'll tell you, as how I always ferves " them there little chits, whenever they begins " to make a noife—I takes them—"

Here the old woman was interrupted by the stopping of the coach at the part of the common where she was to get out and walk to her own house.

Mrs. Barnet warmly recommended the boy to her care, putting at the same time a guinea into her hand, and adding that she would perhaps call upon her sometimes, and would reward her more liberally if she found that the boy was treated with kindness.—The old woman having promised to treat him kindly, led him away, and the coach drove on.

The following morning, Mrs. Barnet, on the pretext of paying an early visit, drove to the old woman's cottage, to inquire after the poor boy.

She soon observed him sitting on a stone before the old woman's door, apart from the other children, who were playing on the heath.

He sprung, with extended arms, towards Mrs. Barnet, as soon as he saw her,

B

" Why are you not playing with the other
" children ?" said she.

" Becaufe," said he, " you promifed to come
" and fee me, and I have watched for you ever
" fince."

" That he has, indeed, madam," said the old
woman, who came out of the hovel, when she
faw the carriage ftop; " he has been conftantly
" on the look-out from morning to night, al-
" though I told him—" You filly fool," said I,
" do you think that that there fine lady, will
" take the trouble to come to fee fuch a poor
" little wretch as you—and what does your
" ladyfhip think he anfwered ?"—

" What *did* he anfwer ?" said Mrs Barnet.

" Yes, I do think it," fays he; " for fhe
" promifed to do fo," said he, " and the parfon
" of the workhoufe fchool told us, that good
" folks always keep their promife," fays he.

" Have you had any breakfaft, my dear ?"
said Mrs. Barnet to the boy.

" I was juft going to give him fome," an-

fwered the old woman, " when your ladyſhip
" arrived.—Was I not, child ?"

" I don't know," ſaid the boy.

" He does not underſtand politeneſs as yet,
" pleaſe your ladyſhip," ſaid the old woman ;
" but I will ſoon teach him in time ; for in-
" deed I was juſt going to give him ſome
" breakfaſt, as in duty bound."

Mrs. Barnet continued to talk with the boy
for a conſiderable time, and was highly pleaſed
with all he ſaid. She then gave ſome money to
the woman, repeating her injunctions, " that ſhe
" ſhould be careful and attentive to the boy ;"
and now, " my dear, here is ſomething for
" you," added ſhe; preſenting him with a large
ſweet-cake.

" Are you going away already ?" ſaid the
boy, with a ſorrowful look.

" Yes, my dear, I muſt go," replied ſhe.

" There," ſaid the boy, giving the cake to
the old woman, " you may divide that among
" the children."

" Firſt take ſome yourſelf," rejoined the old woman ; tearing off a piece, and offering it to the boy.

" No," ſaid he ; " I do not like it *now*."

" You cannot chooſe but like it," ſaid ſhe, taking a large bite of the cake herſelf. " Here, " here," reſumed ſhe, as ſoon as ſhe could articulate ; " I aſſure you it is very nice, ſo there " is a piece for you."

" I cannot eat it now," replied he, rejecting the cake, and looking mournfully at Mrs. Barnet.

" I will come and ſee you again, my dear," ſaid Mrs. Barnet, tapping his cheek ; " but I " am obliged to go at preſent : pray be a good " boy."

" I cannot be a good boy," reſumed he, ready to cry, " when you are going away."

" I will ſoon return," ſaid ſhe, " but pray " be good."

" I will try," ſaid the boy, with a ſob ; " but I fear I cannot."

Mrs. Barnet had not only a warm benevolent heart, but also something of a warm imagination. The accidental manner in which she had met with this boy, and the sudden and growing interest which his appearance, behaviour, and forlorn condition created in her breast, she considered as the impulse of Providence urging her to save a fine boy from vice, infamy, and ruin.

Fraught with this idea, she returned to her own house a little before her husband arose; and by the time he was dressed, she had every thing arranged for his breakfast.

Mr. Barnet entered the parlour with a newspaper in his hand, and, what was seldom the case, with a cheerful countenance.

Mrs. Barnet thinking this the lucky moment for resuming the story of the poor boy—described his fine looks and helpless condition in such eloquent and pathetic terms, that her husband, in spite of his natural indifference to every thing which did not personally regard

B 3

himſelf, ſeemed a little affected.—Mrs. Barnet perceiving this, continued : —

" I do aſſure you, my dear, that you never " ſaw a prettier boy."

" I make no manner of doubt of it," ſaid Mr. Barret ; " but as for the old woman," reſumed his wife, " ſhe ſeemed to be an unfeel- " ing creature, and ſmelt of gin."

" I make no manner of doubt of it," ſaid Mr. Barnet, " for I have known ſeveral old " women ſmell of gin."

" I am ſure ſhe will neglect the poor boy," reſumed ſhe.

" Well, my dear, ſince you are perſuaded of " that, I think we muſt ſend for the old wo- " man, and adviſe her to take care of him ; " and I am willing to give a few ſhillings out " of my pocket for ſo doing," ſaid Mr. Bar- net.

" That would make her *promiſe* to take care " of him," ſaid Mrs. Barnet, " and make her " *appear* very kind to him when you or I are

" with her; but what will become of the poor
" child when we are not prefent?"

" Why, he muft take his chince, like the
" other children," faid the hufband.

" The other children have all fome relation
" to inquire about them," faid Mrs. Barnet;
" but this poor boy is quite deftitute of rela-
" tion, friend, or protector. The poor crea-
" ture himfelf told me that the only friend he
" ever had, died laft week."

" And who was he?" faid Mr. Barnet.

" A poor old foot-man," replied his wife.

" And are you making all this fufs, Jane,
" about a little friendlefs vagabond, whom no-
" body knows?" faid Mr. Barnet.

" If this poor boy were known and had
" friends, he would not ftand in need of our
" protection," replied Mrs. Barnet.

" That is very true," faid Mr. Barnet;
" but, on the other hand, it is very hard on us
" to be the only protector of poor friendlefs
" vagabond boys."

" This is but *one* boy," replied Mrs. Barnet ; " perhaps Providence will never throw
" another fo particularly in our way."

" Why truly, Jane, you furprife me," faid
the hufband ; " you feem to be as much
" concerned about this boy, as if he were your
" own."

" So would *you*, if you had only feen him ;
" he is a moft bewitching little fellow, and al-
" though he is fomewhat pale and emaciated, I
" never in my life beheld a boy with finer fea-
" tures and a more interefting countenance :—
" he brought to my remembrance our own
" poor George, who is dead and gone"—Here
fhe burft into tears, and was unable to fpeak
for a few minutes.

" Pray, do not afflict yourfelf for what can-
" not be helped," faid Mr. Barnet ; " you
" know, my dear, we did all we could for
" George, and the apothecary did all *he* could
" alfo ; he could not have prefcribed a greater
" number of draughts, and cordials, and ju-

" laps, to the only son of a Duke; for his
" bill was as long as a spit, so there is no cause
" for sorrow or reflection.—And as for this
" hospital boy, although he is nothing to me,
" yet since he bears such a resemblance to
" George, I am willing to make a weekly al-
" lowance, out of my own pocket, to the old
" woman, to make her careful of him."

Mrs. Barnet shook her head.

" Why, what would you have me do?" re-
sumed the husband; " you would not surely
" have me take him quite out of the hands of
" the old woman, and be at the whole burden
" of his maintenance myself!"

Mrs. Barnet smiled with a nod of assent.

" Good gracious, my dear! you do not re-
" flect," added the husband, " how strange a
" thing it would be for us to take a poor mi-
" serable wretch of a boy, perhaps the son of
" a foot-man, under our care, and be at the
" whole expence of maintaining him. I should

" be glad to know who will thank us for
" it ?"

" Our own hearts," faid Mrs. Barnet.

" My heart never thanked me for any fuch
" thing fince I was born," faid Mr. Barnet ;
" and I am fure all our acquaintances would
" laugh at us, and turn us into ridicule."

" All the laughters in the world cannot turn
"benevolence into ridicule," faid Mrs. Barnet ;
" and the narrow-minded may be hurt to fee
" you do what *they* cannot imitate; but malice
" itfelf can neither prevent the pleafure which
" a charitable action will afford to your own
" breaft, my dear, nor the refpect which will
" attend it."

" So your drift is," replied the hufband,
" to teafe me till I take this boy into my
" houfe."

" My drift has never been to teafe you, but
" always to make you happy, my dear. I own I
" I am affected with the friendlefs condition of
" this poor orphan, and ftruck with his refem-

" blance to the child who was torn from us at the
" fame age ;—as for the poor young creature's
" maintenance, it will be a mere trifle to us,
" but of infinite importance to him ; it may
" fave him from vice, and the worft kind of
" ruin. The reflection of having done fo cha-
" ritable an office to a lovely boy, like your
" own departed fon, would no doubt afford
" you everlafting fatisfaction : but," continued fhe, perceiving that her hufband began to
be affected, " I defire you to do nothing which
" is not prompted by the generous feelings of
" your own heart ; for of this I am certain,
" that your acting up to them will render you
" more profperous even in this world, and fe-
" cure you a reward of an hundred fold in the
" next."

.. The earneftnefs of Mrs. Barnet's manner, and
the recollection of a fon whom he had loved as
much as he could love any thing, had already
touched the heart of the hufband; and this laft
intimation of immediate profperity and future

reward, founding in his ears fomething like accumulated interest and a large premium, came nearest his feelings, and overcame him entirely.

" Well, my dear," faid he, " fince this is " your opinion, let the boy be brought hither " as foon as you pleafe."

Mrs. Barnet threw her arms around her hufband's neck, and thanked him with all the warmth of an overflowing and benevolent heart.

The China Vafe.

MRS. Barnet had received a prefent of a beautiful piece of china, which fhe valued above its real worth on account of the perfon who gave it.

It was placed with other pieces of china on a chimney piece in the drawing room ; and Mrs. Barnet often gave directions, particularly to her daughter, that it fhould not be removed from its place.

One forenoon during the fummer vacation, Edward fat in this room reading, when Mifs Barnet entered with Mifs Fuller, another young Lady, to whom fhe wifhed to fhow this fine piece of china.

Unmindful of her mother's injunction, " I " will bring it to the window," faid Mifs Barnet to her companion, " and then you will fee " it better."

" Pray, Mifs Louifa, be careful not to let it " fall," faid Edward; " for you know it would " make your mamma fo uneafy."

" That is no bufinefs of yours," faid Mifs Barnet, tartly; and at the fame inftant fhe feized the china with fuch quicknefs and fo little caution, that it flipt from her fingers and was broken to pieces on the hearth.

They all ftood for fome time in filent aftonifhment; but fhe who had occafioned the misfortune was the firft who recovered her prefence of mind.

" Were we all to cry our eyes out," fai

Miſs Barnet, " it would not mend the vaſe ;
" but I have thought of what will ſave us from
" blame."

She immediately ran out of the room, and
returning a few minutes after with a cat in her
arms ; " Be gone into the garden," ſaid ſhe to
the young Lady and Edward ; then throwing
the cat on the floor, ſhe ſhut the door of the
room, and followed them into the garden.—
" Now," cried Miſs Barnet, ready to burſt
with laughter, " my mother will think her fa-
" vourite cat has broken the vaſe—and, if
" ſhe ſhould make any farther inquiry, you
" have only to declare, as I ſhall do," added
ſhe, looking at Edward, " that you know no-
" thing at all of the matter."

" I hope," ſaid he, " that your mother will
" aſk no queſtions of me on the ſubject."

" But in caſe ſhe ſhould, you will tell her
" plainly, that you know nothing about it?"
Edward made no anſwer.

" You will tell her that you know nothing

" of the matter?" repeated Miſs Barnet with a raiſed voice.

" I will tell her no ſuch thing.," ſaid Edward, calmly.

" Why not?" cried ſhe.

" Becauſe, I will not tell a lie," anſwered he.

" Do you mean to ſay that *I* would?"

" I meant to ſay what I repeat, Miſs Louiſa" replied Edward; " that for my own part I will " not.

" Did you ever ſee ſuch a ſaucy compa- " nion?" ſaid Miſs Barnet to Miſs Fuller, as he withdrew.

" O! yes, very often, my dear," replied the other, ſmiling.

" Well, you may laugh as you pleaſe," re- joined Miſs Barnet, " but what he ſaid implied " that he thought me a liar."

" What he thinks, my dear Louiſa, is of little " importance," replied Miſs Fuller; " provid-

" ed we are ourfelves confcious that we are
" incapable of falfehood."

At this remark, Mifs Barnet's face became
of the deepeft fcarlet.

When Mrs. Barnet returned to the drawing
room, fhe faw her favourite vafe lying in pieces on the hearth. The cat rufhed out as foon
as the door was opened; but as Mrs. Barnet
had left Edward reading in the room, and was
certain that no cat was there when fhe left it,
fhe could not avoid fufpecting that he had accidentally broken the vafe, and had afterwards
fhut up the cat in the room to prevent the fuf-
picion from falling on himfelf.—This betrayed
a degree of cunning which fhe did not like, and
of which fhe had never before feen any inftance
in him. She was fenfible that to fome people
a trick of that kind would appear only a proof
of clevernefs in a boy of his age; but fhe had
hitherto confidered him as fuperior to a device
of this nature; and fhe felt, that if it were
clear that he had ftooped to ufe it, fhe never

would be able to efteem and love him as fhe had
done.

She gathered up the fragments of the vafe,
and locked them in her cupboard, without making any inquiry. At dinner fhe remarked that
Edward was graver and more penfive than
ufual, which increafed her fufpicions.

She faid nothing all that day, in the hopes
that he would fpontaneoufly acknowledge what
he had done.

Next day being alone with him, fhe faid a
little unexpectedly, " Pray Ned, do you know
" any thing of the breaking of the vafe which
" ftood on the drawing room chimney ?"

Unwilling to tell what he knew, and confufed with the queftion, he made no anfwer.

His uneafinefs and confufion confirmed her
fufpicions.

" When I left you reading in the room, the
" vafe was whole, was it not ?" faid fhe.

" Yes it was," anfwered he.

" You were alone," refumed fhe ; " there

" was *not so much as a cat* in the room with
" you when I left it," added she.

Greatly diftreffed at this remark, the boy
feemed more and more confufed.

" Accidentally breaking a piece of china,"
continued Mrs. Barnet, " is a trifle ; the means
" which feem to have been ufed to conceal it,
" I view in a different light, and it gives me
" pain to think that thofe I love are capable
" of artifices which betray cunning at the ex-
" pence of candour."

. Edward wiped the tears from his eyes, but
faid nothing.

" I thought you too wife and manly to be
" cunning," continued Mrs. Barnet.

The boy feemed much diftreffed

" Perhaps," refumed Mrs. Barnet, " you
" wifh to give fome explanation of this mat-
" ter."

" I can give no explanation," faid he, in a
voice half fuppreffed with anguifh ;—" but—
" but—Oh! I am very unhappy."

" Nay, my dear," said Mrs. Barnet, moved
by the distress in which she saw the boy;
" there is no need to be *very* unhappy; it was
" natural for you to imagine I should be un-
" easy at the loss of the vase, and you could
" not bear, I suppose, to be thought the cause
" of my uneasiness.—I am sure such a thought
" would give you pain."

" Indeed it would," said he, in a voice hard-
ly articulate.

" When such an accident happens again, be-
" lieve me, my dear, your best course will be
" to avow it honestly, without racking your
" invention for devices to conceal it."

Having said this, Mrs. Barnet left him in
more uneasiness of mind than he had ever felt
before.

It cost him a severe struggle to bear the idea
of her displeasure; but when he reflected that
he could not do himself justice without ac-
cusing the daughter of his benefactress, and
conveying to the mother's breast more vexation

than she felt in thinking him blame-worthy, he determined to remain silent, and actually returned to school without giving the least hint on the subject.

Miss Barnet's resentment against Edward increased, he had made her look mean in her own eyes. She felt therefore a disagreeable sensation as often as his name was mentioned. Perhaps she was incapable, coolly and considerately, of doing an essential injury to this boy; but the painful sensation which she felt when she thought of him, made her without design speak of him sometimes in an injurious stye, and at one time in the hearing of her mother.

Mrs. Barnet hinted at the unfairness of taking advantage of his absence to insinuate any thing to his prejudice; adding, that Edward was incapable of speaking against people in their absence.

" What is nearly as bad, however," replied the daughter; " he is capable of speaking with " insolence and injustice to people *in their pre-* " *sence.*"

" Edward is as incapable of the one as the
" other ;" said Mrs. Barnet.

" He told me the other day, in pretty plain
" terms, that I was a liar," said the daughter.

Miſs Barnet gueſſing by her mother's look
that ſhe did not believe her, ſaid, " Miſs Ful-
" ler was preſent when he did ſo."

Mrs. Barnet reſolved to inveſtigate the truth
of the accuſation ; and for that purpoſe, ſhe
called one forenoon on Miſs Fuller, and aſked
whether ſhe had ever heard Edward ſay any
thing unbecoming to Louiſa. The young lady
declared ſhe never had. " He may have been
" provoked to it," reſumed Mrs. Barnet, " but
" I have reaſon to think he behaved with ſome
" degree of inſolence in your preſence." Miſs
Fuller now recollected what had paſſed when
the vaſe was broken, and related the whole
candidly as it had paſſed.

Mrs. Barnet's mind was now divided between admiration of Edward's conduct and un-
eaſineſs on account of her daughter's.

After she had gratified her natural difpoſition to redrefs an injury, and communicate pleaſure by writing to Edward, ſhe remembered that the painful duty of remonſtrating with her daughter remained unfulfilled. Afraid, how-ever, of the effeςt which ſtating her conduςt in the heinous light which it appeared to her-felf might have on the young lady's mind, ſhe ſpoke to her in the following terms :

" I find, my dear, that you entirely miſtook
" what Edward ſaid, when you deſired him to
" conceal from me the accident by which the
" vaſe was broken. It was not unnatural, how-
" ever, in you to be provoked with any ex-
" preſſion that could poſſibly be conſtrued into
" ſo foul a reproach as that of lying—the miſ-
" apprehenſion of a ſentence has often led peo-
" ple of the beſt diſpoſitions and intentions into
" error; for, on a very narrow baſis of miſtake,
" a vaſt ſtruςture of falſehood may be raiſed to
" the ruin of the moſt meritorious charaςter.
" The quicknefs of your temper, my dear

" Louifa, led you into an error, in repeating
" to me what Edward faid, which might have
" made an impreffion highly injurious to his
" character, had it not been prevented by my
" obtaining a real ftate of what paffed from
" your friend Mifs Fuller, who is fo partial to
" you as to take the whole blame of breaking
" the vafe on herfelf, declaring that it proceed-
" ed from her impatient curiofity to fee it. and
" your eagernefs to gratify her. The lofs of
" the vafe, however, gives me little or no un-
" eafinefs ; but had it given me a great deal,
" it would have been entirely difperfed by the
" fatisfaction of finding that Edward has not
" behaved in the manner that ftruck you, and
" that you are incapable of *wilful* mifprefenta-
" tion."

Had Mrs. Barnet ftated her daughter's conduct in the worft light, the young lady was of
a temper to have attempted a juftification ; and
what we once are led, or provoked to juftify,
we are apt to repeat: whereas, inftead of at-

tempting any defence or apology, Mifs Barnet was fo much affected with the delicacy of her mother's remonftrance, that fhe ftood fpeechlefs, with her eyes fixed on the ground, which Mrs. Barnet obferving, gently fqueezed her hand and left the room. Mifs Barnet was no fooner alone than fhe burft into tears, and continued weeping for a confiderable time.

Her heart informed her, that her conduct did not deferve the palliations it had received; and although nothing pleafed her fo much, in general, as her mother's praife, yet, on the prefent occafion, it rather diftreffed her, becaufe fhe was confcious fhe did not deferve it.

The Shrove-Tuefday Cock.

THERE was a cock at Harry's nurfe's, the lord of the dunghill, between whom and Harry a very particular intimacy and friendfhip had been contracted. Harry's hand was his daily caterer; and Dick, for the cock was fo called, would hop into the child's lap and pick his clothes, and rub his feathers againſt him, and court Harry to tickle, and ſtroke, and play with him.

Upon a Shrove-Tueſday, while Harry was on his road from his patron's, intending a ſhort viſit to his nurſe and foſter-father, a lad came to the door and offered Gaffer a double price for Dick; the bargain was quickly made, the lad bore off his prize in triumph, and Gaffer withdrew to the manuring of a back field. Juſt at that criſis Harry came up, and inquired of the maid for his daddy and mammy, but was anſwered that neither of them was within. He then aſked after his favourite cock; but was, told that his daddy had, that minute, ſold him to yonder man, who was almoſt out of ſight.

Away ſprung Harry like an arrow from a bow, and held the man in view till he ſaw him enter a great crowd, at the upper end of the

C

ftreet. Up he comes, at laft, quite out of
breath, and making way through the affembly,
perceived his cock, at fome diftance, tied to a
fhort ftake, and a lad preparing to throw at
him with a ftick. Forward he rufhed again,
and ftopped refolutely before his bird, to ward
the blow with his own perfon, at the inftant
the ftick had taken its flight, and that all the
people cried out, Hold! hold! One end of the
ftick took Harry in the left fhoulder, and bruif-
ed him forely; but not regarding that, he inftantly ftooped, delivered his captive favourite,
whipt him under his arm, caught up the ftick,
flourifhed it, as in defiance of all opponents,
made homeward through the crowd, and was
followed by the acclamations of the whole affembly.

The old gentleman was ftanding before his
court-door when his favourite arrived all in a
fweat: What's the matter, my dear, fays he;
what made you put yourfelf in fuch a heat?
what cock is that you have under your arm?

In anſwer to theſe ſeveral queſtions, Harry in-
genuouſly confeſſed the whole affair; and, when
his patron, with ſome warmth, cried, Why,
my love, did you venture your life for a ſilly
cock? Why did I? repeated the child; why,
Sir, becauſe he loved me. The old gentleman
then ſtepping back, and gazing upon him with
tender eyes of admiration; May Heaven for
ever bleſs thee, my little angel, he exclaimed,
and continue to utter from thy lips the ſenti-
ments that it inſpires. Then catching him up
in his arms, he bathed him with his tears, and
almoſt ſtifled him with his careſſes.

The Fool's Coat.

THERE was, once upon a time, a very
good and a very clever boy called Hercules. As he grew up, beſide his prayers and
his book, he was taught to run, and leap; to
ride, wreſtle, and cudgel; and though he was

able to beat all the boys in the parish, he never
used to hurt or quarrel with any of them. He
did not matter cold, nor hunger, nor what he
eat, nor what he drank; nor how, nor where
he lay; and he went always dressed in the skin
of a wild beast, that could bear all winds and
weathers, and that he could put on or off at
pleasure; for he knew that his dress was no
part of himself, and could neither add to him,
nor take away any thing from him.

When this brave boy came to man's estate,
he went about the world, doing good in all
places; helping the weak, and feeding the
hungry, and clothing the naked, and com-
forting those that cried, and beating all those
that did hurt or wrong to others; and all good
people loved him with their whole hearts, and
all naughty people feared him terribly.

But, O sad and dismal! a lady, whom he
had saved from great hurt and shame, made
him a present of a new coat, which was called
a shirt in those days, as they wore it next the

ſkin. And now, take notice. The lady had covered his coat, all over, with laces, and with rufflings, and with beads of glaſs, and ſuch other fooleries; ſo that poor Hercules looked juſt as fine as you do now. And he turned him to this ſide, and he turned him to that ſide, and he began to think more and better of himſelf, becauſe he had got this fool's coat upon him. And the poiſon of it entered into his body and into his mind, and brought weakneſs and diſtempers upon the one and the other. And he grew ſo fond of it, that he could not bear to have it put off; for he thought that to part with it, would be to part with his fleſh from his bones. Neither would he venture out in the rain any more; nor box nor wreſtle with any body, for fear of ſpoiling his fine coat. So that, in time, he loſt the love and the praiſes of every body; and all people ſcorned him, and pointed at him for a fool and a coxcomb, as he went by.

C 3

The Nutting Party.

AUTUMN was now advanced, and Richard with his brother, a number of little affo-ciates, and an attending footman, got leave to go to the copfe a-nutting. As the children were perfectly acquainted with the way, the fervant defired to ftay behind a while, in order to provide hooks for pulling down the branches. This was granted, and forth they all iffued in high chat and fpirits.

The copfe lay at fome diftance, on one fide of the park behind the manfion-houfe; but, when they had nearly approached the place of their deftination, Harry miffed a garter, and, promifing fpeedily to rejoin his companions, went back to feek it.

In the mean time his affociates, on entering the wood, met with another little poffe of the village-fry, who were on their return, one of whom carried a bag of nuts that feemed bulkier

than the bearer. So, Gentlemen, fays Richard,
where are you going? Why, home, where
fhould we go? fays a little boor, fullenly. And,
pray, what have you been doing? fays Richard.
Guefs, fays the boy. Is it nuts that you have
got in that bag? demanded Richard. Afk to-
morrow, anfwered the boor. Sirrah, fays
Richard, a little provoked, how dare you to
come, and pull nuts here, without our leave?
Why, as for that, Mafter Dicky, replied the
other, I know you well enough, and I wouldn't
afk your leave, an' you were twenty lords, not
I. Sirrah, fays Dicky, I have a great mind to
take your nuts from you, and to give you as
good a beating into the bargain, as ever you
got in your life. As for that, Mafter Dicky,
coolly anfwered the villager, you muft do both
or neither. Here I lay down my nuts between
us; and now come any two of you, one down
t'other come on, and if I don't give ye your
bellyfuls, why then take my nuts and welcome,
to make up the want.

This gallant invitation was accepted on the
fpot. Richard chofe his companion in arms,
and both appeared quite flufh and confident of
victory. For, though neither of them had
been verfed in the gymnaftic exercifes, they
didn't want courage, and they knew that the
challenger was their inferior in ftrength and in
years.

Richard began the affault, but was down in
a twinkling. To him his friend fucceeded, but
with no better fortune. A fwing or trip of
Tommy's fent them inftantly to gather ftrength
from their mother earth. And though thefe
fummer-heroes were forely intent on defend-
ing their pretty faces from annoyance, yet
Tommy at the third turn had bloodied them
both.

Harry, who was now on his return, perceived the engagement, and running up, and
rufhing between the combatants, interpofed
with a voice of authority, and parted the fray.

Having inquired, and duly informed himfelf

of the merits of the cafe, he firft turned him to Richard, and faid, O brother Dicky, brother Dicky, you ought not to hinder poor boys from pulling a few dirty nuts, what fignifies 'em? Then turning to the challenger, his old acquaintance; Tommy, fays he, did you know that Dicky was my brother? Yes, fays Tommy, rudely, and what though if I did? O, nothing at all, fays Harry, but I want to fpeak with you Tommy. Whereupon he took the conqueror under the arm, and walked away with him, very lovingly in all appearance, looking about to take care that none of the boys followed him.

Coming to a fmall opening, in a fecreted part of the wood, Harry quitted his companion, defired him to ftrip, and inftantly caft afide his own hat, coat, and waiftcoat. Why fhould I ftrip? fays Tommy. To box, fays Harry. Why fhould you box with me Harry? fure I didn't ftrike you, fays Tom. Yes, Sir, replied Harry, you ftruck me when you ftruck Dicky, and knew that he was my brother. Nay, Harry, cried Tom, if 'tis fight you are for, I'll give you enough of it, I warrant you.

Tom was about eight months older than Harry, his equal in the practice of arms, and much the stronger. But Harry was full as tall, and his motions, quicker than thought, prevented the ward of the most experienced adversary.

Together they rushed like two little tygers. At once they struck and parried, and watching every open, they darted their little fists, like engines, at each other. But Tom, marking the quickness, and feeling the smart of Harry's strokes, suddenly leapt within his arms, bore him down to the earth, and triumphantly gave him the first rising blow.

Harry rose, indignant, but warned, by the strength of his adversary, to better caution. He now fought more aloof; and as Tom pressed upon him, he at once guarded, struck, and wheeled, like an experienced cock, without quitting the pit of honour.

Tom finding himfelf wholly foiled by this method of combat, again rufhed upon his enemy, who was now aware of the fhock. They clofed, they grappled, they caught each other by the fhoulders, joined head to head, and breaft to breaft, and ftood like two pillars, merely fupported by their bearing againft one another. Again they fhifted the left arm, caught each other about the neck, and cuffed and punched at face and ftomach, without mercy or remiffion; till Tom, impatient of this length of battle, gave Harry a fide-fwing, and Harry giving Tom a trip at the fame time they fell fide by fide together upon the earth.

They rofe and retreated, to draw breath, as by mutual confent. They glared on one another with an eye of vindictive apprehenfion. For neither of them could now boaft of more optics than Polyphemus; and, from their fore-

C 6

head to their fhoes, they were in one gore of blood.

Again they flew upon each other, again they ftruck, foined, and defended, and alternately preffed on and retreated in turns, till Harry, fpying an open, darted his fift, like a fhot, into the remaining eye of his enemy. Tom, finding himfelf in utter darknefs, inftantly fprung upon his foe, and endeavoured to grapple; but Harry, with equal agility, avoided the fhock, and traverfing here and there, beat his adverfary at pleafure; till Tom cried out, I yield, I yield, Harry, for I can't fee to fight any more.

Then Harry took Tom by the hand, and led him to his clothes, and having affifted him to drefs, he next did the fame friendly office to himfelf. Then, arm in arm, they returned much more loving, in reality, than they fet out, having been beaten into a true refpect and affection for each other.

Some time before this, the footman had join-

ed his young Lord, with the feveral imple-
ments requifite for nutting. They had already
pulled down great quantities ; the young qua-
lity had ftuffed their pockets, and the little vil-
lagers, who had affifted, were now permitted
to be bufy in gathering up the refufe. When
all, turning at the cry of There's Harry, there's
Tom, they perceived our two champions ad-
vancing leifurely, but hand in hand, as friends
and brothers.

They had left their clothes unbuttoned for
the benefit of the cooling air; and as they approached, their companions were frozen into
aftonifhment, at the fight of their two friends
all covered with crimfon.

They were neither able to advance to meet
them, nor to fpeak, when they arrived. Till
Richard firft inquired into this bloody cata-
ftrophe, and Harry, remaining wholly filent
on the fubject; blind Tommy cried out, Why,
Mafter Dicky, the truth is, that Harry beat
me, becaufe I beat you. Then Dicky, feeling

a sudden gush of gratitude and affection rising
up in his bosom, looked wistfully on his brother, and said, with a plaintive voice, O brother Harry, brother Harry, you are sadly hurt;
and, turning about, he began to weep most
bitterly. But Harry said, Shaw! brother
Dicky, don't cry, man, I don't matter it the
head of a brass pin. Then turning to the
footman, with Tom still in his hand, he cried,
Here, John, take that bag of nuts and poor
blind Tommy to my mammy's, and tell daddy
that I desire him to see them both safe home.

Benevolence to Animals.

I HAPPENED to be staying with my friend Mr.
Barnet during the vacation; Edward, who
was then about twelve years of age, met a man
in a field near the house with four or five
dozen of larks: the boy having amused himself by looking at them fluttering about in the

basket, asked the man what he intended to do
with them? and being told that he was going
to sell them, " What will become of them
" then?" said the boy. " They will be roast-
" ed and eaten," said the fellow. On which
the boy began to bargain for the birds, merely
for the pleasure of saving their lives, and giving them their liberty.

He produced all the money he had, and offered it for the birds ; but the man refused, say-
ing he was sure of getting more from a gentleman who was very fond of roasted larks.
" Roasted ! Poor little pretty creatures !" cried
the boy, looking compassionately through the
basket. " Pray, good friend, let me have them ;
" I will bring you more money, when I re-
" ceive my next month's allowance."—" I'll
" be hanged, if I trust you," said the fellow ;
" get along," giving the boy a rude push : but
as he had hold of the cover of the basket, it
was raised by the push so much, as to allow
one-half of the birds to fly away ; and when

2

the man endeavoured to force down the cover, Edward kept his arm between it and the edge of the basket, until all the remainder escaped. The boy's arm was severely squeezed, and his face much bruised, for the man continued to beat him after the struggle; and he would have suffered more, had not a servant maid of Mr. Barnet's, who had been witness to the whole scene, interfered: His face and eyes were so much swelled and inflamed, and he was so feverish next day, that the man absconded; but Edward getting well in a few days, stopped the prosecution that was intended, and went and paid to the man's wife, out of his allowance, the full price her husband had demanded for the birds.

Mr. Barnet, as a Justice of the Peace, told him that the man having taken revenge without applying to the laws of the land, had no right to any other indemnification: but Mrs. Barnet approved of what Edward had done from first to last, and she insists upon it, that

the voice of the lark will now found more a-
greeable in his ears than ever.

Can there be any comparifon between the
pleafure Edward will have in hearing fuch
creatures rejoicing in the fky, with that which
an epicure feels when he fees them in a difh ?

The Ufeful Difappointment.

ONE fine morning, in the month of June,
Ambrofe prepared to fet out with his father on a party of pleafure, which for a fort-
night before had taken up all his thoughts.
He had rifen, contrary to his cuftom, very
early, in order to haften the preparations for
his jaunt. However, juft as he thought that
he had reached the object of his wifhes, the
fky darkened all at once, the clouds grew thick,
and a violent wind bent down the trees and
raifed up a tempeft of duft. Ambrofe went
down every moment into the garden, to ob-

ferve how the fky looked : he then fkipped up
the ftairs three at a time, to examine the barometer ; but the fky and the barometer were
both againft him. For all this, he did not
fcruple to give his father good hopes, and to
affure him that thefe unfavourable appearances
would difperfe in a moment ; that prefently it
would be the fineft weather in the world ; and
he concluded, that they ought to fet out directly, to have the benefit of it.,

Mr. Powell, who did not repofe a blind con-
fidence in his fon's prognoftics, thought it more
prudent to wait a little. Juft then the clouds
burft, and difcharged a heavy fhower of rain.
Ambrofe, who was doubly difappointed, began
to cry, and obftinately refufed to be comforted.
The rain continued until three o'clock in the
afternoon. At length the clouds difperfed, the
fun refumed its luftre, the fky its clearnefs,
and all nature breathed the frefhnefs of the
fpring. Ambrofe recovered his good humour
by degrees, in proportion as the fky brighten-

ed. His father took him out a little way, and the calmnefs of the air, the finging of the birds, the frefh green of the fields, and the fweet perfume that breathed all round him, reftored peace and fatisfaction completely to his heart. Do not you remark, faid his father to him, the agreeable change juft now produced all around you? Recollect how dull every thing yefterday appeared to us ; the ground parched up by a long drought, the flowers without colour, and hanging ther languid heads ; and in fhort, all vegetation feeming to be at a ftand. What muft we fuppofe to have fó fuddenly made nature appear young again ? The rain that has fallen to-day, faid Ambrofe.

The injuftice of his complaints, and the folly of his behaviour, ftruck him fenfibly as he pronounced thefe words. He blufhed, and his father judged that his own thoughts would be fufficient to teach him another time to facrifice, without reluctance, a felfifh pleafure to the general advantage of mankind.

Moral Precepts.

NO knowledge can be attained, but by study.

If you would be free from fin, avoid temptation.

Loofe converfation operates on the foul, as poifon does on the body.

Do to others, as you would have others do to you.

Be more ready to forgive, than to return an injury.

Never excite thofe thoughts in others, which will give them pain.

If you would be revenged on your enemies, let your life be blamelefs.

He muft be utterly abandoned, who difregards the good opinion of the world.

Religion does not require a gloomy, but a cheerful afpect.

Your countenance will be agreeable, in proportion to the goodnefs of your heart.

None can be a difciple of the graces, but in tie fchool of virtue.

As you value the approbation of Heaven, or tle efteem of the world, cultivate the love of vrtue.

Be armed with courage againft thyfelf, againft thy paffions, and againft flatterers.

Riches, honours, pleafures, fteal away the heart from religion.

Forget not, that the brighteft part of thy life is nothing but a flower, which is almoft as foon withered, as blown.

Prepare for thyfelf, by the purity of thy mamers, and thy love of virtue, a place in the happy feats of peace.

Perform your duty faithfully; for this will procure you the bleffing of Heaven.

Make a proper ufe of your time; for the lofs of it can never be retrieved.

Enjoy pleafure; but enjoy it with moderation.

Use no undecent language; for indecency is want of sense.

Sport not with pain and distress; nor us the meanest insect with wanton cruelty.

Be not proud; for pride is odious to God and man.

Never value yourself upon your fortune; for this is the sign of a weak mind.

Envy not the appearance of happiness n any man; for you know not his secret griefs.

Murmur not at the afflictions you suffer; for afflictions may be blessings in disguise.

Apply thyself to learning: it will redound to thy honour.

Read the scriptures: they are the dictates of divine wisdom.

Fear God: he is thy Creator and Preserver.

Honour the king: he is the father of his people.

Harbour no malice in thy heart: it will be a viper in thy bosom.

Be upon thy guard against flattery: it is a delicious poison.

Avoid affectation : it is a contemptible weak-
nefs.

Do not defpife human life : it is the gift of
God.

Do not infult a poor man : his mifery en-
titles him to pity.

All manki d want affiftance : all therefore
ought to affift.

Cherifh a fpirit of benevolence : it is a god-
like virtue.

A tear is fometimes the indication of a noble
mind : JESUS WEPT.

Philofophical Obfervations.

EVERY leaf, every twig, every drop of
water, teems with life.

In the leaft infect there are mufcles, nerves,
joints, veins, arteries, and blood.

Chance never produced lions, tygers, bears,
ftags, bulls, fheep, dogs, or horfes.

Vapours are formed into clouds, dew, mift, rain, fnow, hail, lightning, and other meteors.

The colours in the rainbow are violet, indigo, blue, green, yellow, orange, red.

The earth is adorned with a beautiful variety of mountains, hills, valleys, plains, feas, lakes, rivers, trees, flowers, plants, and animals.

A Moral Leffon.

TRUTH is the bafis of every virtue. It is the voice of reafon. Let its precepts be religioufly obeyed. Never tranfgrefs its limits. Every deviation from truth is criminal. Abhor a falfehood. Let your words be ingenuous. Sincerity poffeffes the moft powerful charm. It acquires the veneration of mankind. Its path is fecurity and peace. It is acceptable to the Deity. Bleffed are the pure in heart.

THE END.